1421 MAPLE

A STARLITE MYSTERY

THE STARLITE SUPERNATURAL MYSTERY SERIES

RAY & MICHELE FRASER

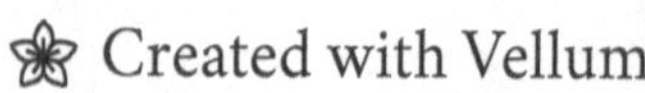 Created with Vellum

*This book is dedicated to all the
wonderful neighbors in the world
like John, Diane, Rita, Hani, and the kind
souls who always try to lend a helping hand.*

May you never have a neighbor like Mr. Crow

ONE

It was a big lot, almost a double. Certainly, large enough to build a house on. To Jimmy Michaels, it was a link to happiness. Jimmy lived in the house right next door to the flat, vacant lot. Fourteen twenty-one Maple had seen many baseball, football, and field hockey games. In the winter, Jimmy's dad would hook the hose to the outside faucet, and create an ice rink for Jimmy and all of his friends to skate on. Jimmy had enjoyed the use of the space for the full ten years of his life. Now, that was all about to end.

The first indication came when the men

arrived with the gizmos that stood on three legs, and had a telescope on top.

"They are surveyors," his dad had said. "It looks like they are going to develop the property."

The thought of losing his playing field hit Jimmy very hard. The nearest park was almost three blocks away. His parents would never let him go all that way on his own. Also, the other kids in the neighborhood were older than Jimmy, and it meant they would no longer have a reason to play with him.

Even after the surveyors left, Jimmy and the neighborhood boys continued to play on the lot. They simply pulled the sticks with the orange streamers out of the ground, and moved them out of their way. Things took a decided turn for the worst the day the excavator arrived.

Jimmy was awakened on that June morning by men shouting and swearing outside his bedroom. Sleepily, he went to the window and looked outside, his tousled blonde hair sticking up in all directions.

A big, burly man, with a tattoo of a

woman on his forearm, stood right beneath his window, holding one of the sticks with an orange streamer.

"Damn kids." He stormed, breaking the stick in two and hurling the parts to the ground.

Jimmy stepped back away from the window where he could not be seen, and watched as the burly man and a skinny fellow with bucked teeth, took a tape measure and tried to match the measurements with something they looked at on a rolled-up paper.

Finally, after about two hours of measuring, they started the motor on the digger. There was a period of excitement as the shovel took the first scoop of what was to be the basement of the new home, but that quickly faded. Where were they going to play now? After a few moments' reflection, Jimmy put on his Detroit Tigers t-shirt, his favorite jeans, and his Air Jordan tennis shoes, and headed into the kitchen.

"Good morning, honey. Did you sleep well?"

Jimmy sat on his seat at the side of the

table, and rubbed the remaining sleep from his eyes. "I guess so."

Tammy Michaels looked at the small round face of her son. His blue eyes were sullen. His usually smiling mouth was sad. She knew something was up.

"What's the matter?'

"Nothin'."

"Nothing? That's a pretty sour face for nothing."

"Can I have some oatmeal?"

Jimmy was generally the first one up and out of the house. Breakfast was something that almost never slowed him down. Today, he seemed unhurried.

"Sure, honey. Oatmeal it is. How come you aren't running outdoors to play?"

"Cause, they're digging up the lot next door. There's no place to play."

Tammy knew this was eventually going to happen. Even so, she was unprepared to deal with the level of disappointment she saw in her son's face.

"Honey, you knew that sooner or later they were going to build a house on that lot. It's one of the nicest ones in Brampton."

Jimmy didn't answer, but instead stared down at the table. In the distance, he could hear the soft murmur of the digging machine. The only thought that lingered in his mind was that his life was over.

When at last he had eaten his breakfast, he asked Tammy a fateful question. "Mom, where am I gonna play now?"

Tammy finished wiping the table and placed the dishes in the sink before responding. "Well, we still have our back yard and Tommy has his. When you want to play baseball, we can go to the park."

Jimmy knew that's what she would say. What else could a mom say? Their back yard was small. Like Tommy's, their lot was one of the smallest in the subdivision, and their houses took up most of the space. There was also the fact that his mom had just taken a job in Carmain, and would be gone till at least an hour after he got home from school each day.

There would be no park, no baseball or football games. The best he could hope for would be that his dad would still freeze the yard for ice skating in the winter. Stupid house, anyway.

After watching the latest episode of *Stranger Things*, Jimmy decided to go out to the front porch and watch the work going on next door. Just as he opened the door, Tommy rode up on his bike.

"Hi, Jimmy."

"Hi, yourself."

Tommy Jacobs knew why Jimmy was upset. Since he had just arrived, the full impact of what was taking place at 1421 Maple had not yet sunk in for Tommy.

"Looks like they're building a house on our lot."

Jimmy didn't look at Tommy. Instead, he stared at the excavation. "Du-u-u-h-h-h-h," he said rudely. "How'd you notice?"

Tommy and Jimmy had been friends almost since the day Tommy's family moved into the brick house at 1651 Maple. Tommy was older, but he and Jimmy shared many of the same interests. Tommy knew what the house meant. He also knew that being two years younger than himself, Jimmy would be restricted as to where he could play.

"We can still play in the back yard and you can come to my house."

This time Jimmy turned to look at Tommy. "Yeah, right."

Tommy had his head virtually shaved, with a wisp of hair down the center, combed upward, and secured with setting gel. His slender face and dark eyes reflected the Italian heritage of his mother.

Over the next half hour, Jimmy and Tommy watched silently as the hole got bigger and deeper. Every once in a while, the burly man would glance menacingly in their direction. Jimmy would glare right back, as though he were unintimidated by the man's surly behavior.

"Tommy, you want a sandwich?"

"Sure. What kind do you got?"

Jimmy opened the front door to the house. "I don't know. My mom will fix something up." Then, glancing back at the excavating at 1421 Maple, he added, "Stupid house, anyway."

The boys walked into the kitchen where Tammy stood loading the dishwasher.

"Hi, Tommy."

"Hello, Mrs. Michaels," Tommy responded.

"Mom, can we have a sandwich?"

"Sure, honey. What kind do you want?"

"I want a double-decker PBJ."

"What do you want, Tommy?" she asked.

"That's fine with me." He smiled.

"Two double-decker peanut butter and jelly sandwiches, coming up," Tammy said. "Honey, get Tommy and yourself a coke from the fridge."

Tammy enjoyed being the neighborhood mom. All the kids felt comfortable in their home, and they all treated her and Roy with respect. She had always wanted more than one child, but childbearing had been hard on her, and after Jimmy was born, she and Roy decided that if they wanted another child, they would have to adopt. That was nine years ago, and now she had pretty much resigned herself to being the mom away from home for the neighborhood kids.

Tammy set the sandwiches on the table

in front of the boys and pushed back a strand of blonde hair which had fallen over her face.

"If you want another, just let me know," Tammy said, before walking back to the kitchen sink.

"Mom?"

"What, honey?"

"Is there anything we can do to stop them from building the house next door?"

Tammy smiled, revealing beautiful straight white teeth. "No, Jimmy, I don't think so. Who knows, maybe the family that is moving in will have children your age. You could make a new friend. Why not just wait and see what happens."

That was an angle that Jimmy hadn't considered. If the family had kids, the lot was still big enough to do something on. Maybe it wouldn't be so bad after all.

Over the next few weeks, Jimmy and the rest of the neighborhood boys watched the house develop. First, it was the pouring of cement walls for the basement. Jimmy thought that was neat. Next came the carpenters. They woke him early one Saturday with their hammering and sawing. Today would be the day they put in the floor. Jimmy rushed downstairs to watch from the porch.

By now, the workmen had grown used to having Jimmy and his friends around. The boys were courteous and stayed out of their way as the men worked on the house. Jimmy had even come to know some of them by name.

One of the important ones, a man named Kurt, occasionally had Jimmy help out on the job, fetching water for the men, or relaying a message or two. At the end of the day, Kurt would always reach into the worn pockets of his work jeans and pull out a dollar for Jimmy. He hoped Kurt would need help today.

"Hi, Jimmy."

"Hi, Kurt," Jimmy responded, feeling very important to be noticed.

"You want to make a buck?"

Jimmy flew off the porch and over to lot 1421, filled with anticipation. "What do you want me to do?"

"Well, Mr. Crow, the new owner, is

coming by today to check on our progress. When he gets here, let me know. He drives a green car."

"Okay," Jimmy answered enthusiastically.

Just before lunch time, Jimmy saw the green car turn off of Apple Street, and on to Maple. He quickly jumped up and ran to find Kurt.

"Kurt, he's here. Mr. Crow is here."

"Thanks, Jimmy. While Mr. Crow and I talk, why don't you check with Jeff and see if he needs your help."

"Gotcha," Jimmy said, and ran off to talk to the other foreman.

After fetching water for the crew, Jimmy was leisurely returning the glasses to his house. He was just about to leave the property when he heard the gruff voice.

"Who the hell is that?"

Kurt turned to look at Jimmy. "The kid? Oh, that's Jimmy. He lives next door. Nice kid. He helps out around here from time to time. I give him a buck. It's an easy way for him to earn some spending money."

"Kurt," Mr. Crow began, "I got no use for

kids. Period. Don't have him back on this job site, or I'll get another crew to finish the job." Then glaring at Jimmy, he added, "You just stay on your side of that line, boy. Mrs. Crow and I don't need you traipsin' all over our property with your delinquent friends."

Kurt's face burned. He wanted to set Mr. Crow straight, but he knew this was not the time nor place.

Mr. Crow's tirade had cut Jimmy deep. Any hope he had of making a new friend was squashed with those cutting words. This would be the darkest day in a long time. Now, not only had he lost his play area, he'd also lost hope.

TWO

"Honey, it's almost time for supper."

Jimmy lifted his head from the pillow. He'd been asleep most of the afternoon and couldn't remember the last time he'd cried so hard. He felt so lost. No play area, and eventually, no friends. Even though his dad said that boys aren't supposed to cry, he didn't understand; this was different.

After washing his face and hands, Jimmy looked into the mirror. He felt relieved. You could tell he'd been sleeping, but you couldn't tell he had been crying.

At the dinner table, Jimmy was happy to see a big bowl of spaghetti. His mom hadn't prepared it for a while. At least for the moment, it made him forget the troubles brought on by 1421 Maple. Jimmy set his fork down after finishing his second helping, and wiped his mouth on the yellow cloth napkin his mother had bought to match the kitchen.

"Dad?'

"What, son?"

"Are we gonna move any time soon?" The ache in Jimmy's voice indicated a deep concern.

"Why do you want to move?"

Jimmy shrugged. "I don't know. I was just askin', that's all."

Roy loved his son dearly. Jimmy had been born on his thirtieth birthday. Jimmy was the spitting image of his father, and Roy had never felt love for anyone, even his wife, like he felt for his son Jimmy. It was as if there were a special, unwritten bond between them.

Roy took a deep breath before answering, "I know you wouldn't be asking about moving unless something made you unhappy. What's on your mind?"

Jimmy shrugged again. "Well, since they started building that stupid house next door, the only friend that comes down anymore is Tommy, and there's no place to play when he's here. I hoped I might get a new friend when they finished the house, but I met the owner today, Mr. Crow, and he told me to go home and stay off his property. I wasn't even doin' anything except helping Kurt."

Roy had met the construction foreman, and had thanked him for his interest in Jimmy. A little work, a little financial reward, and before you knew it, Jimmy would be a responsible person.

There were at least two concerns. First, if Mr. Crow didn't like children, he was moving into the wrong neighborhood. Theirs was a subdivision that consisted of young families. Secondly, if Mr. Crow was as mean-spirited as Jimmy had indicated, Roy was concerned about what it would be like to live next door to him.

"Well, son, I know it sounds tough now, but we'll get this all worked out. I'll talk to Kurt tomorrow and see if I can't meet Mr.

Crow. He may not be such a bad guy after all."

Jimmy was unconvinced. "You didn't hear him, Dad." Then Jimmy screwed up his face into a sneer before continuing, "Stay on your side of the line, boy. I don't need you traipsin' all over with your delinquent friends."

Roy could sense the anguish in Jimmy's words. He walked over to where he sat and put his hand on Jimmy's small shoulder, giving it a loving squeeze.

"We'll work it out, son. I promise."

The next day dawned bright and sunny. Even before Roy was dressed, he could hear the construction crew getting ready for their day's work. This would be a good time to talk to Kurt.

"Kurt, how you doing?"

"I'm fine, Roy," the foreman answered, taking off a heavy work glove and shaking hands.

"Looks like it's coming along."

Kurt nodded. "Yeah, it is. I've got a couple of workers off today, so I have to pitch in. How's Jimmy?"

Roy shook his head. "That's what I want to talk to you about. I guess he had a run-in with Mr. Crow yesterday."

Kurt nodded again. "It wasn't a run-in, Crow just jumped on his case as soon as he saw him. If I didn't need the job, I would have set him straight. Heck, Jimmy works harder than some of my crew." He laughed. "You know, some people are just never happy. Crow seems like one of those."

"Do you think it would help if I talked to him?"

"Well, talkin' can't hurt. I don't see it doing any good with Crow, but you can try."

"Next time he's coming around, will you let me know?"

"Sure thing. And, tell Jimmy if he wants to come to work, we'll have something for him to do and he'll get paid. Crow always calls before he comes. We'll keep it as our little secret."

The men shook hands again. "Thanks for your help, Kurt."

As Roy walked back into the house, Jimmy was standing just inside the door.

"What'd he say, Dad?"

"Well, the first thing he said was that you could come back to work if you wanted. I'm also going to talk to Mr. Crow and see if maybe he wasn't just having a bad day."

"Can I go now?"

"Sure, son. Go earn some spending money."

Before Roy had even finished the sentence, Jimmy was on his way off the porch, and running towards the lot which now held a partial structure that would soon be a house at 1421 Maple.

It was just before five thirty when Roy turned into the short drive and parked the Dodge Caravan. It had been a good day. Life in the world of running your own business was tough. Today, however, business had been brisk, and the customers were friendly and knowledgeable. That was somewhat of a rarity.

Since opening Hardware Central, he had invested most of his extra cash and all of his free time in the business. At last, after five years of effort, it was beginning to pay off. His mind toyed with the idea of a real vacation for his family. He was brought back to reality by the sight of Jimmy sitting on the glider near the edge of the porch.

"Hi, Tiger. How was your day?"

Jimmy sat up and made room for his dad to sit down. "Oh, it was good. I helped Kurt most of the day, and when he said I looked like I was getting tired, he gave me the rest of the day off. Today, I made five dollars —look."

Jimmy reached in his pocket and pulled out the neatly folded bill.

"I did water, and ran messages, and he even let me carry some of the wood for the floor. He said I did a real good job, and that you would be proud of me."

Roy leaned over and gave his son a hug around the shoulders. "I am proud of you. You're a good worker, and someday you'll earn real money for your work."

Jimmy was unimpressed. "Dad, I said I earned five dollars," he responded, emphasizing the words, *five dollars*. "That is real money."

Roy chuckled, "You did good, son. Just

be sure and save at least some of your money."

"Dad?"

"What, son?"

"Kurt said that Mr. and Mrs. Crow are coming over before six o'clock. Do you think you could talk to them and see if they have kids or grandkids I could play with?"

"Sure. We may find out that they aren't such bad people after all."

"I don't know," Jimmy began, "he seemed pretty mean to me."

At promptly five fifty, the green car turned onto Maple Street and pulled in front of the construction site. The squat, rotund man with thinning hair, exited the driver's side of the vehicle, adjusted his pants, and walked over to where Kurt stood waiting.

"You're behind schedule," he began gruffly.

"Good evening, Mr. Crow. It's good to see you again," Kurt responded, ignoring his verbal barrage.

"Don't get smart mouthed with me. You know the schedule."

"Mr. Crow, until the move-in date has past, I'm not behind. I promised it would be done on time, and my record speaks for itself. All you need to worry about is being ready to move in when the house is complete. How is Mrs. Crow?"

The dumpy man turned and looked at the woman silhouetted behind the darkened glass of the tinted car windows. He ran his hand across his chin.

"I'd suspect that right about now, she's upset because you're behind schedule."

Kurt smiled and waved at her image and thought he perceived a wave in return. As he focused his attention to Mr. Crow, they were joined by Jimmy's dad.

"Hello, Mr. Crow, I'm Roy Michaels. I guess we're going to be neighbors. So, I thought I'd introduce myself."

Mr. Crow looked at Roy Michaels' outstretched hand, but didn't shake it.

"Michaels, we may live next to each other, but we aren't going to be neighbors. Don't come around here butting your nose into my or my wife's business. And, keep that brat kid of yours on your own property."

Roy Michaels' face flushed red with anger, as he let his hand fall back to his side. He realized that Kurt couldn't say anything, though the look on his face said volumes. He figured that since he was going to live next door to this guy, now was as good a time as any to set things straight.

"Okay, Mr. Crow, if that's how you want to start out your life in this neighborhood, so be it. Your attitude will bring you what you deserve, but be very careful. I spent three tours of duty in Iraq and I'm not afraid of dealing with people like you. If you threaten my son or my family in any way, you'll be very unhappy with my response. If you so much as look at Jimmy crossways, I'll be sure that you know exactly how close he and I are." Then with a disgusted look and a cynical tone he added, "Welcome to the neighborhood."

Benjamin Crow was undaunted, looking eye to eye with Roy. After a moment's stare down, Roy started to walk away. He paused for a second, not turning around as the grumpy man spoke.

"Just mind your own business and we won't have a problem."

Roy Michaels silently continued his walk back home. Once inside, he went to the restroom and splashed cold water on his face. *What a jerk,* he thought. *I felt like kicking his butt.*

Over the next few months, construction on the house at 1421 Maple moved along according to schedule. Roy Michaels had seen Benjamin Crow a few times, but it seemed odd, he never saw his wife.

Kurt had said the house was ahead of schedule, and that the couple would move in sometime in November. As much as Roy tried to put things in the proper perspective, his mind crept back to the day in early summer when Mr. Crow had challenged him.

As the house neared completion, the amount of time that Jimmy spent helping Kurt also diminished. With the word out that Mr. Crow was a mean person, the other neighborhood boys had decided that

Jimmy was a liability. Because they were older, they were able to go to the park to play, and that left Jimmy out of the loop. As time went on, he become more and more withdrawn and depressed.

On a sunny Saturday morning in early September, Tammy Michaels decided it was time to approach the issue with her husband. She was deeply concerned. Jimmy had just started back to school and was having problems. At home, he stayed to himself, often in his room for hours on end. His eating and sleeping habits had become erratic. Jimmy was becoming a troubled child.

"Roy, I don't know what to do. Jimmy's not eating well, he never smiles, and his attitude has changed. Why, the second day of school he even got into a fight. That's not like Jimmy."

Roy agreed. "I'll talk to him, today. Maybe we can get him to loosen up."

"I sure hope so. I'm worried. We need to nip this in the bud before it gets worse."

"Sweetheart, I said I'd talk to him. I'll do it today, I promise."

They had just finished their conversation when Jimmy walked into the kitchen.

"Do you want some breakfast, honey?"

Jimmy shrugged. "I guess so."

"What would you like?"

Jimmy slumped into one of the chairs at the kitchen table and took a deep breath and sighed. "I don't know."

"Would you like some pancakes?"

Jimmy nodded without looking up. "I guess."

Tammy glanced at Roy. He immediately picked up on her signal.

"Jimmy, I've got some time off today. How would you like to go to Belle Isle and do some fishing?"

For the first time in many days, Jimmy sprang back to life. "Do you mean it?"

"Of course."

Jimmy was ecstatic. He wolfed down the pancakes and dashed to his room to get dressed. Today would be a very special day.

Belle Isle was an island park in the middle of the Carmain River. Roy had been going to the island since his early youth. On days just like this one, his father would often take him fishing there. They always had a picnic, and if they were lucky, they brought home a few fish to eat.

Roy's father had also grown up going to the island. "Back then," he used to say, "we didn't have no bridge to drive across. You rented a boat at the livery and rowed across." It was usually about that time he would start into the story of how he and Ida Baker went fishing against his father's wishes. While on the island, "the worst storm in a hunert years blew in and we was forced to stay on the island over night."

Roy laughed to himself and shook his head, remembering the punishment his grandfather had meted out to his dad. Oh, well, he thought, there would be no storm today, only some good fishing and some good conversation with his son.

He finished the last sip of coffee and placed the cup in the sink. Tammy was already busy making sandwiches and packing the small cooler for the day. Roy went to the garage to be sure all the fishing tackle was in order. They would stop at Annis' Market and pick up a few minnows and some night crawlers. Fishing was the activity of the day, but the purpose was to see if Jimmy could get back to his happy-go-lucky self.

"I'm ready, Dad."

Roy looked up and got a lump in his throat. Jimmy had dug deep into his closet to find his grandfather's fishing hat, which now sat wrinkled and perched at an angle on top of his son's head. He choked back his emotions.

"Me, too, son. See if your mother has our lunch ready while I put our tackle in the car."

Jimmy was gone in a flash. A minute or two later, he reappeared carrying the small white cooler, filled to the brim with sandwiches, snacks and cool drinks.

"I think we got everything," Jimmy said after dutifully placing the cooler in the trunk and standing back to survey the gear.

Roy smiled. "Perfect. I'll tell your mother good-bye, and we'll be on the road."

Jimmy didn't get to sit in the front with his dad too often. Most of the time, that spot was reserved for his mother, and

Jimmy was relegated to the back seat. This was certainly going to be a great day.

After a short stop for bait, they were on their way across the bridge to Belle Isle.

"Do you think we'll catch anything?"

Roy thought for a minute then smiled at his son. "Sure we will. The worms have given me their word. Besides, your mom said she wasn't sure what to fix for supper. We'll just have to supply the food."

Jimmy was satisfied. He hoped his dad would let him pick the spot to fish from. He felt lucky today and was sure he could pick a place where they could catch their limit.

"So, where are we going to fish today?"

Jimmy beamed. "How about the lighthouse? We always do good there."

"The lighthouse it is."

Over the next few minutes, Jimmy refreshed his memory on how to bait a hook using a worm or minnow. This time his dad had also bought some crickets. He'd never used one before, but figured he would be able to learn without too much trouble.

Finally, their cushions were placed, their hooks baited, and father and son sat beneath the shade of a large oak tree that leaned over the edge of the water, casting wonderful shadows for the fish to hide in. The patient wait had begun.

To Roy's surprise, Jimmy had not made a comment about the house at 1421 Maple. They had talked about the upcoming hockey season and Jimmy's first tryout with a travel team. Because the ice rink that his dad made every year was so close to his house, Jimmy had become an avid skater and hockey player. He started out playing in the beginner's league and was now ready to take the next step.

After the conversation about hockey subsided, Roy decided to broach the issue of the Crows and their house. He began cautiously.

"Have you seen the progress on the Crows' house lately?"

Jimmy answered solemnly, "Yeah, Kurt says it will be done in a few weeks. I guess Mr. Crow is there almost every day."

"Has he said anything else to you?"

Jimmy shook his head. "Uh-uh. I stay out of his way when he comes around. You know he doesn't even look at me when I'm sitting on the porch."

"Well, son, he may not be such a bad egg after all. Maybe we just have to get to know them."

Jimmy was silent for a few minutes. "Dad, what's a sorcerer?"

Roy laughed. "Why?"

"Tommy said that Mr. Crow is probably a sorcerer and that Mrs. Crow may be a witch and they're gonna turn all of us kids into frogs or something."

"Well now, that is an interesting question. A sorcerer is a male witch that specializes in magic. But don't listen to those stories that Tommy made up. Witches and sorcerers aren't real, at least I don't believe they are."

Jimmy was obviously not convinced.

"Why'd they have to move into our neighborhood? There's vacant land on Poplar Drive and Willow. Did they have to pick our field?"

Roy sighed. "Well, you first have to realize that it was never our lot. Besides, it's a big one. Big enough to build a house on and still have a nice yard."

Roy waited a few moments before moving in to the part of the conversation he'd wanted to address since they left home.

"I know it bothers you that they've built a house on that land."

Jimmy didn't reply for a few moments. When he finally did, he answered as though he were thinking it through. "Yes and no. I'll be skating with the team and won't need the rink as much, but Mr. Crow is so mean, I'm hoping you and mom will start letting me go to the park instead of waiting till next year. I don't wanna go that long without friends."

Jimmy had obviously considered his options. For now, he was alone. Only Tommy came to hang out, and for the most part, they just watched the crew build the house, or helped Kurt.

After a moment of silence, Roy spoke. "Okay. Let's assume that eventually they move into the house. When they do, you get one wish, what would it be?"

Jimmy answered almost instantaneously.

"I wish the ground would open up and suck Mr. Crow and his stupid house off my lot so I can get my friends back."

Roy was stunned. "That bad, huh?"

Jimmy continued without looking up, "And, if she really is a witch, it can suck her up too."

For the first time, Roy knew exactly how his son felt. The harshness of his words left no question as to the pain he had accepted at the loss of his play area. He also knew that such thoughts weren't healthy for a young boy to have. They would need more conversations about the situation. For now, he decided he would try and diffuse Jimmy's feelings.

"Well, maybe after they move in and we get to know them a bit, things might change. It does happen, you know?"

Jimmy was unimpressed. "Yeah, and he could get meaner, too. I just wish he'd move someplace far away and leave us alone."

The conversation would have to continue later. For now, nature was calling, and Roy was hearing the voice. "Can you watch my pole while I go to the john?"

"Sure," Jimmy said in his most responsible voice. "I'll take care of everything."

The bathrooms were just over the rise in the landscape. Only a short distance away, but placed so that Roy could not see his son from them. He trusted Jimmy to be responsible and presumed that if he hurried, he could be back in just a minute or two. He headed for the hill.

"Catch anything?"

Jimmy looked into the face of the blonde-haired, blue-eyed little girl. "No, not yet, but we will. Me and my dad always catch something here. What's your name?"

"I'm Sanora."

"That's a different name."

"Not where I come from. It's quite common. What's your name?"

"My name's Jimmy. Where'd you come from?"

Sanora turned, pointing to the base of the tree. "Over there."

"Huh. You said where you come from your name is common. Where's that?"

Sanora smiled, the wind gently blowing the curls of her short hair. "Oh, not far away, but you wouldn't recognize it if I told you."

Jimmy seemed satisfied. "Are you here with your folks?"

"They're around here somewhere. I couldn't help but hear your wish. This Mr. Crow doesn't seem like a nice person."

Jimmy noticed that Sanora seemed grown up for her age.

"He's mean and he hates kids. He took the only lot on Maple to build his stupid house and now I have no friends."

"Would you like him to go away?"

"And how," Jimmy answered quickly. "Far away, once and for all. Maybe then I could get my friends back."

Sanora reached her hand into the pocket of her jeans and pulled out a folded paper. "When you're ready for him to leave, do what it says on this sheet, but be careful. Be very sure you want him gone."

Jimmy took the paper and stuffed it into his own pocket without opening it. He started to say something, but Sanora raised her finger to her lips in a shushing fashion and continued, "What kind of fish do you like?"

"I like walleye best."

Sanora passed her hand slowly in an arc. In only a second, his pole snapped and bent towards the water. It was obvious he had a fish on the line. Momentarily, his attention was focused on reeling it in.

Roy was back. "Looks like you got one."

"Boy, you're here just in the nick of time. He's a big one."

Roy reached to help his son. As the fish neared the shore and the open net, he thought to himself, *that's the biggest walleye I've ever seen.* Just as the fish was placed in the storage cooler, Roy's line bent under the weight of a sizable catch.

The next half-hour was spent landing fish, one after the other, until their limit was reached. Roy looked into the cooler. These were trophy walleye. Almost every one was a near-record size. In all of his years of fishing in the Carmain River, he'd never even seen one walleye as big as these. Now, he had a cooler full.

"Looks like we'll be eating good tonight," Roy said.

"I'm starving now," Jimmy replied.

"Let's clean up and eat some of the food your mother fixed."

For the first time since he started catching fish, Jimmy noticed Sanora was missing. "Dad, did you see a little girl here when you came back?"

Roy shook his head. "No, I didn't. Why?"

Jimmy related the story of Sanora's appearance, and pulled the folded paper from his pocket.

Roy opened it up, however the entire page was blank. "There's nothing on this paper."

Jimmy examined the paper, turning it over in his hands. "Wow! I wonder what she meant?" He then carefully folded the paper back to its original size and returned it to his pocket. "That was cool. I thought I saw writing on it when she gave it to me."

"Well, it's gone now, son. Maybe it was a joke or a trick."

"She asked me what kind of fish I liked. I said walleye, and boy did we catch 'em."

Roy now took a different look at their bounty. Yes, they had caught walleye. In fact, they'd caught nothing but walleye. That was unusual for the Carmain River.

After a filling lunch and some animated conversation about the town's professional hockey team, Roy and Jimmy headed toward home. On the way, they stopped at Annis' Market.

Annis Joseph was Roy's baseball coach and mentor from many years before. Annis had decided to retire from his regular job, and get close to what he loved the most, fishing. At his little market you could get just about anything you wanted or needed for the sport. Most days if you arrived before noon, he was out fishing and his son was running the store. Today, he was in.

"Well, that's the darnedest thing I've ever seen. These are some mighty big fish," Annis said after surveying their catch. "Most would be trophies. Where'd you say you caught 'em?"

"By the lighthouse."

"Ain't no walleye by the lighthouse. You

may catch a stray, but mostly there's trout and bluegill."

"I know. That's what I thought, too. But, that's where we were. You want one for your supper?"

"Sure thing," Annis said, laughing. "Me and the missus will have some good eatin' tonight."

When Roy and Jimmy pulled into their drive, the Crows were standing on the sidewalk in front of their new house. Mr. Crow was shaking a finger in Kurt's face. As they walked to the door, Roy could hear his gruff voice warning Kurt.

"This house had better be according to plan, Mr. Richards, or you won't be paid a cent. Do you hear me?"

Kurt replied, "I hear you, Mr. Crow. Now, if you and your wife want to go in and look around, we can get started on the finishing touches."

As Roy and Jimmy stood at the door, Mrs. Crow turned her head in their direction. Roy almost dropped the cooler of fish when their eyes met; they were stunned at her youth and beauty. Thinking of the rotten personality exhibited by Mr. Crow, they surmised that there was no possible way this woman could be his wife.

They noticed she looked at least twenty years younger than him, and while he was short and pudgy, she was lithe and vibrant. She looked more like she could be his daughter. Her reddish blonde hair hung just past her shoulder and glistened in the sunlight. In short, Mrs. Crow was stunning.

Roy walked into the kitchen, setting the cooler on the granite counter next to the sink. Tammy came in from the living room.

"Hi, guys."

"We've got good eatin' tonight," Roy exclaimed proudly.

Tammy had heard this before. Usually, when Roy brought home fish, there were one or two fair-sized and the rest were runts. This meant fixing up a number of side dishes to complement the meal. This time when she opened the cooler, her mouth fell open in astonishment.

"My god. These are the biggest fish I've ever seen. Where did you catch them?"

"That's what Annis said, too. We caught

them by the lighthouse. He said there weren't many walleye there." Roy shook his head. "I guess he was wrong about that."

"I caught the first one," Jimmy boasted.

Roy smiled. "That he did and it was the biggest catch of the day."

Jimmy beamed from ear to ear. Certainly, there would be no special need to for extra sides tonight.

With his stomach full of fresh fish, macaroni and cheese, bread, and chocolate cake, Jimmy was ready for a little quiet time. He adjourned to his room. Throughout supper, he could hear Mr. Crow yelling at Kurt as they walked through the new house.

Jimmy assumed that Mr. Crow didn't realize the sound carried quite well in this quiet neighborhood, and with everyone's windows open, their business would be the business of all within earshot. After thinking about it for a while, Jimmy wondered if maybe he didn't care that people heard. He sure was a grouchy man.

It was near bedtime, and Jimmy was tired. He was ready to put his pajamas on and settle down. While undressing, he reached into the pocket of his jeans and pulled out the folded piece of paper. To his amazement, there were faint markings. Not so clear that they could be read, but certainly clear enough to see. These marks had not been visible when his dad looked at the paper earlier. What was it Sanora had said?

When you're ready for him to leave, follow the directions on this paper. Jimmy carefully refolded the paper, and then placed it in his secret hiding space behind the board that hid the plumbing system to the bathroom. Even his mom didn't know about this spot.

Over the next month, little happened. Kurt spent a great deal of time inside the house making it just so. Mr. Crow had come by a time or two to check on the progress, but Jimmy had only caught glimpses of him coming and going. He never did see Mrs. Crow again.

The Saturday before his birthday, Roy had arranged for them to go fishing again. This time, Jimmy got to pick the place.

"I want to go back to Belle Isle, if that's okay."

"Sure, Tiger. Wherever you want to go."

That Friday, Jimmy was sitting on his porch, watching the landscapers place the sod that would become Mr. Crow's yard. Kurt came out of the house, closed the door, and surveyed the progress. His eye caught Jimmy sitting on the porch.

"Hey, Jimmy, how's it going?"

Jimmy jumped off the porch and went to where Kurt stood watching the crew.

"Fine," he said, approaching the muscular man. "How's the house coming?"

Kurt laughed. "That's a good question. For anybody else, the house is done, for Mr. Crow—I don't have a clue. For all I know, he could tell me to tear it down and start over."

Jimmy nodded, thinking. "Kurt, did you ever see his wife?"

Kurt's head turned away from watching the landscapers. "Sure, she was the younger strawberry blonde woman with him when he came to see the house that one time. Why do you ask?"

Jimmy shrugged. "I don't know. She just

didn't seem like his wife. I mean, did she look like his wife to you?"

Kurt laughed loudly. "How old did you say you were?" Then laughing again. "No, Jimmy, she did not seem like his wife. She's different, too. There's just something about her. Who knows? Maybe they're made for each other."

"So, are you done?'

"Yep. He's gonna come by and give it a final look-see, and then I get paid, and he moves in. I feel sorry for the neighborhood. Everyone seems like such nice folks." Kurt mused for a moment and then shrugged. "Maybe he'll change."

Jimmy wasn't so sure. "I don't think so."

"Me, neither. He doesn't seem like the kind. I wish you good luck in dealing with him though."

Saturday came and went without event. Jimmy and his dad went to the Carmain River and fished all day. They caught the normal amount of trout and bluegills, but they didn't catch a single walleye.

The ritual for the day mirrored that of the previous visit, and when Roy left to go to the restroom, Jimmy hoped Sanora would return. He was disappointed when she didn't. He had questions he wanted to ask her about the paper and about herself. Maybe she would be there next time.

When Jimmy finished eating supper, as was a frequent custom, he stepped out to the porch to sit on the glider, in hopes that his friends would come by and want to hang out, even though he knew they wouldn't. Now that the intrigue of a new house under construction had passed, Jimmy was pretty much alone.

He was reminded of what Kurt had said. *Maybe he'll change.* Well, Jimmy resolved, changing that grump would not bring his friends back to the end of the street. He hated that stupid house.

As Jimmy sat, the movers were just bringing in the final pieces of furniture. He thought, *I might as well watch, there's nothing else to do.* He was in a daydream state, not really even paying attention to the movers, when he heard the booming voice.

"What the hell do you think you're looking at, you nosey little brat?"

Jimmy was startled. "Uh, nothing, Mr. Crow. I was just sitting on my porch."

"Well, look somewhere else until we get our stuff moved in. If I want the whole neighborhood to know what kind of furniture I have, I'll hold an open house. I sure don't need a snotty-nosed kid like you spreading the news for me."

Jimmy stuttered, "B-b-but, I wasn't really looking."

Roy heard the commotion and came out onto the porch. "What seems to be the trouble here, Mr. Crow?"

"Trouble? That little private investigator of yours is taking notes as to what we have in our house. No doubt, so he can break in and steal it when we're not home."

Roy couldn't believe his ears. "You're kidding, right?"

Benjamin Crow turned beet red. "Kidding? No, Mr. Michaels, I'm not kidding. Fourteen twenty-one Maple will be an armed house. Remember it."

Then, spinning on his heel, he turned and went back. After a few steps, he stopped, turned again to face them and added, "Be sure your brat kid remembers it, too."

The tension in the air was like a dense fog. Jimmy sat speechless on the glider. His dad took a deep breath and sat down next to his son.

"Jimmy, I don't know why Mr. Crow is like he is, but try not to take it personally. He's a sick man. Somehow or other, we'll figure out a way to deal with him."

Tears welled in Jimmy's eyes. He hated him, hated his house, and now he was even beginning to hate his neighborhood.

"Dad, can we move?"

"Move? We're not going to move because of that man. He has no reason to be the way he is. I promise, we'll figure it out."

"It's not just him. All I do is sit on this stupid glider. I was just thinking, if we moved somewhere else, maybe I could make some friends again."

Roy Michaels felt his son's pain. What could he do? What *would* he do? Only time would tell. Later, he and Tammy would have to work on plan to keep Jimmy happy, and to keep Mr. Crow on his side of the property.

About two weeks after the move in, Tommy came by to play football with Jimmy. They didn't have a big yard to play in, so for a while, they passed the football on the sidewalk in front of Jimmy's house.

"Go deep," Jimmy said before launching the football in the direction of the Crows' property line. Before the ball had even reached Tommy, he saw the stumpy man standing near the edge of the house. Jimmy's throw was a good one. Too good, in fact. It sailed over Tommy's outstretched fingertips before taking a sideways bounce and rolling into the Crows' yard. Tommy carefully began to step onto the grass to retrieve it when he heard the bellowing voice.

"You take one step onto the grass, you little insect, and I'll have you arrested for trespassing. Now, get the hell off my grass."

Jimmy decided to take the polite approach. "Mr. Crow, we're sorry the ball bounced into your yard. We'll be more careful next time. May we please have it back? It's my favorite ball."

The heartless man took a few steps and picked up the ball. Then, mimicking Jimmy's plea, he repeated, "It's my favorite ba-a-a-l-l-l. You should have thought about that before you tossed it into my yard. Now, get off my sidewalk before I call the cops."

Jimmy quickly turned and ran back to his house. Tommy followed, waiting patiently on the porch while Jimmy explained the event to his mother. Then he came out and sat across from Tommy on the railing.

"This totally sucks!

"He's a jerk," Tommy exclaimed.

Jimmy nodded. "I agree! He's like that all the time. My mom says my dad will get the ball back when he comes home from work. I guess we'll have to practice later."

THREE

At five twenty-five, as was his custom, Roy walked through the back door, kissed his wife on the cheek, and was given the news of the day's events. *What is that man thinking?* He mused. *He must have a screw loose or something. But, no time like the present to get the situation resolved.*

"How long till dinner, dear?"

"Fifteen minutes."

"Come on, Jimmy. Let's go get your ball."

After several rings of the doorbell, the heavy, white, wooden door swung open, and Mrs. Crow stood facing them behind the storm door. She made no attempt to open it.

Roy had never seen her up close. She looked to be in her mid-twenties with clear skin, and a shapely figure. It was odd that such an attractive woman would be married to a person like Mr. Crow. But, as they say, love is blind.

"Is your husband in?"

Mrs. Crow hadn't opened the door, nor had she greeted them in any way. She said nothing, only turned and walked down the hall to the rear of the house. After a few moments, the silhouette of Benjamin could be seen in the hallway. In an instant, he was at the door.

"What do you want, Michaels?"

"We'd like to get my son's football back."

"Oh, you would, would you?" He continued, sneering, "If he wants to keep his ball, then keep it off my property. If you really want it back, here it is." He reached behind the door, picked up a plastic shopping bag and threw it at them shouting, "Now get off my porch before I call the cops."

Jimmy picked it up. Inside, his favorite football had been cut into little strips. He dropped the bag on the porch and ran home to the security of his room. Roy grabbed the bag and headed home. On his way, he thought, *enough was enough. Maybe the police could help.*

"I don't know, Roy," Officer Campbell began. "He sounds like a kook, but if the ball was on his property, he does have his rights. I don't agree with his use of them, but there's not much I can do. I'll talk to him and be back in a few minutes."

Police Corporal Tracy Campbell had been Roy's friend since high school. Roy didn't know what else to do. He hoped Tracy would be able to give him a hand.

"Well?"

Officer Campbell shook her head. "Well, is right. They're both weirdos. He wouldn't open the door unless I had a warrant. I told him to call us next time if there was a problem, or I would encourage you to file a damage complaint. I got to see his wife, too. Ugliest woman I've ever seen."

The football situation took a back seat.

"Ugly? His wife is gorgeous. Strawberry blonde hair, nice eyes, smooth skin. You're pulling my leg, right?"

Corporal Campbell looked straight at Roy and laughed. "Please tell me that you're kidding me. The hair is right, but she's a wrinkled old hag. She looks just as bad as he does."

"There must be another woman. I saw her. She was a knock-out."

Officer Campbell shrugged. "You may be right. He wouldn't agree to call us, but I warned him not to damage anything else. Keep your ball in your own yard, kiddo. It'll be easier that way."

As Jimmy got ready for bed that night, he looked down from his window, to the house at 1421 Maple.

"I hate you, Mr. Crow," he said. "I hate you, and I wish you'd never moved here."

In the window below, he could see the back of Mrs. Crow. She appeared to be rocking in large circles, listening to some rhythm. Over and over, she would rock one way, and then back the other. Probably some stupid witch's ritual, he figured. Maybe she really was a witch. As he peered through the glass, he thought he heard a faint voice. The hair on the back of his neck stood straight up and the voice whispered again, "I'm watching you."

Just then the doorbell rang and startled Jimmy. He went to run downstairs to see who it was, but tripped on a shoe, lost his balance, and almost fell to his doom. Luckily, he caught the banister just in time. When he reached the door, his father was talking to one of the neighbors.

"Have you seen Cookies?" It was Mrs. Rogers.

"No, ma'am," Jimmy began. "Not since I was at your house. Is he missing?"

Cookies was the Rogers' family cat. A big fluffy animal with fur the color of caramel. He looked just like a big, hairy, sugar cookie. He was the friendliest cat Jimmy had ever known, snuggling up to anyone willing to pay him some attention. Jimmy hoped he was safe.

"He went out last night to do his business and never came back. It sure isn't like him to run away."

Jimmy nodded. "If I see him, I'll bring him home and also ask Tommy to be on the look out."

"Thanks, Jimmy. We appreciate anything you can do."

Roy closed the front door. Since the Crows had moved in, the whole neighborhood seemed unhappy. Beginning with the loss of the field, his football, and now the Rogers' cat was missing. Jimmy didn't know how, but he bet that Mr. Crow was responsible. Maybe Cookies went into his yard or something.

Although he tried to rest after hearing the news, he bounced between sleep and wakefulness, as nightmares about the disappearance crept into his mind.

"Want to go fishing?"

Jimmy struggled to open his eyes. It was Saturday and the weather was supposed to be beautiful. It would be a great day for fishing. His dad was all set to go, having dressed, fixed lunch, and packed the car.

Jimmy jumped up and quickly grabbed his clothes. "Can we go to Belle Isle again?"

"Sure, son," Roy replied. "We can go anywhere you like."

After a piece of toast and an apple, Jimmy was anxiously waiting for his dad to open the car. Before he heard it unlock, he looked back towards 1421 Maple. On the porch of the house stood Mrs. Crow. She was the most beautiful woman Jimmy had ever seen. Why had Officer Campbell thought she was ugly?

The day of fishing was perfect. Jimmy quickly caught his limit of trout and was scanning the wooded area near the fishing site. *I wish she would come back*, he thought. Why had Sanora given him the paper? Why couldn't he ask her questions?

Roy sat quietly facing the water, his line dangling near the rocks, in an attempt to catch at least one more big one. After that, he said, they could go home. Jimmy sat on the bench near the edge of the river, playing with a spider web that had been spun in the crook of the bench.

"Spiders are beautiful creatures."

Jimmy's head snapped up. It was Sanora. "Dad, this is the girl I was telling you about." Roy didn't stir.

"He can't hear us."

"Why not?"

"Some things are better if they're private. I see the Crows are giving you more trouble. Are you ready for them to leave yet?"

"I've been ready! He wrecked my favorite football. He probably also killed Mrs. Rogers' cat. Plus, his wife is weird. When me and my dad saw her, she was beautiful, but when Officer Campbell saw her, she was as ugly as a toad. Today I saw her and she's pretty again. She also does this thing where she rocks and sways in a chair like she's listening to music, but I don't ever hear music. She's strange."

"She's also dangerous, so be careful. There are things in our universe that you don't understand yet, but I promise you, you don't want to end up like Mrs. Rogers' cat."

"So, what should I do?"

"A man will come to your house and speak with your father. He'll tell him things about the Crows that he won't believe, even though they're true. Your dad will be so surprised that he won't tell anyone about it, but if you ever ask him, he'll tell you. Before then, there will be a deep sadness in the neighborhood. Then it will be time for you to use the paper."

With that said, Sanora turned and walked back into the woods. At the moment she disappeared from view, Roy turned to face Jimmy.

"Well, sport, it doesn't look like I'm going to be lucky. Why don't we just head home?"

That night at supper, the family dined on fresh fish. As Jimmy was finishing his last french fry, he asked his dad if he'd seen Sanora.

"Sanora? That little girl you said was there a while back? No, I didn't notice her. I must have been daydreaming. What did she want?"

Jimmy started to answer, but before the words could come to his lips, he felt the urge to say, "Oh, nothing. She was just wondering how our luck was."

"I hope you showed her your catch." Roy thought back. "Wasn't she the same girl that came around the day we caught the walleyes?"

"Uh-huh."

"Well, we should invite her more often. She seems to bring us good luck."

"May I be excused, please?"

"Sure, going to get ready for bed?"

Jimmy nodded. "I'm kinda tired."

Jimmy had just closed the door to his room when there was a faint knock at the front door.

"I'll get it," Roy told Tammy, heading for the door. As he opened it, he saw a man in casual clothes standing on the other side.

"Yes?"

"Mr. Michaels, my name is Thadius Williams. I'm an associate of Sanora's."

Roy recognized Sanora's name. "Oh, yes. Jimmy's friend from the river. Come on in."

Thadius shook his head. "No, thank you. This will only take a minute."

Roy turned to look at Tammy. She sat motionless, staring straight ahead. At that moment Roy felt a sense of understanding come over him. He slowly turned back to Mr. Williams.

"What is this about?"

"Your son Jimmy is the key to eliminating a significant force of evil that is located right here in your neighborhood. The Crows are not who they seem. I've been advised that you've already felt the ire of their dark energy, as has Jimmy. These are wicked people. They have escaped the lower realms and must be returned. That's where Jimmy comes in. As an ancient spirit, he has the power to send them back to their rightful place. Over the next hour, he will perform an incantation with the help of Sanora, and your neighborhood will be cleansed of the darkness."

Roy shuttered. "Are you some sort of an angel or something?"

"Let's just say, Roy, there are powers in the universe that are greater than both of us."

"So, why tell me?"

"Jimmy's future is preordained. He has a destiny in this existence that must be fulfilled. This is merely the first step."

"Okay, so why tell me?" Roy repeated.

"Jimmy will need a confidant. Your wife is a wonderful woman, but she will never understand. As Jimmy grows, memories will come to you that will be of ancient powers and rites. Jimmy will have these same memories. You must help him achieve his calling."

"What do you want me to do, just go up to him and say Jimmy, I've had this really neat conversation with an angel-guy, and he says you are to be some great protector of the world?"

Thadius laughed. "I'm glad to see that you haven't lost your sense of humor. No, it will actually be easier than that. The day will come, in approximately six of your years, when Jimmy will ask you about this conversation. Until that time, you won't be able to talk to anyone about it. Any memories you have of it, will be cast aside as unbelievable. Also note that Sanora will become a close friend of Jimmy's soon after he enters high school. You'll remember her, but you won't recall from where, until after Jimmy's sixteenth birthday. I must go now. We will meet again."

Roy closed the door and turned to look at Tammy. For the first time since the doorbell rang, Tammy looked in his direction.

"Who was it?"

"Uh, just someone selling magazines. I told them we didn't need any."Then hoping to change the subject, he added, "Here, let me help you with the dishes."

What a weird experience, Roy thought. *Could it all be true? Do sinister people really come into a neighborhood to build houses?* He reasoned not. *It must have been a trick, or a dream*, he imagined, shaking his head.

He wondered if Tammy had seen what he saw.

"Dear, did you see the person at the door?"

"No, why?"

"Well, it was …" Roy's voice trailed off. He tried to gather his thoughts, but none came. He struggled in vain. Realizing that the effort was futile, he concluded, "Nothing really, just curious."

CHAPTER

FOUR

A ritual had already begun by the time Jimmy was ready for bed. Mrs. Crow sat on the same chair, near the table, rocking, swaying, chanting an unheard mantra. This time, she seemed more animated and intense.

Jimmy sat quietly in his room. The lights were off to prevent the Crows from seeing him watching. This pattern had been going on for many months now and was becoming more frequent. In all of his observations, Jimmy had never seen Mr. Crow included in the activity. Jimmy silently wondered what he was doing when Mrs. Crow was rockin' and rollin', as he called it.

As things were rising to a crescendo, he felt his heart racing. Just then a loud knock on his door caused him to jump.

"Jimmy? Tommy's here. He wants to talk to you."

"Okay. Tell him I'll be right down."

Jimmy stood up and just before he turned to leave the room, he took one last look at Mrs. Crow. For only a split second, she had her head thrown back and he could clearly see her face. She was the ugliest person he'd ever seen, all gnarled and wrinkled. Her nose bulbous and protruding. He would have to let Tommy see this.

"Did you hear?"

"Hear what?"

"The Franklins. Their baby was stolen. Someone went right into their house and took him. The cops suspect it's some kind of an adoption ring. It was on the news today."

"Do they think they'll find him?"

Tommy shrugged. "Geez, I don't know. I sure hope so. He was a cute kid."

"Can you stay a minute?"

"Sure, but not too long."

"Come up to my room, there's something I've got to show you."

Tommy thought it was strange that Jimmy didn't turn on the light in his room. Instead, Jimmy placed his finger in front of his lips in the shushing fashion and got down on his hands and knees and crawled over to the window. Tommy followed suit.

When they reached the glass, Jimmy whispered, "Look."

Tommy peered through the window, down into the Crows' house. There sat Mrs. Crow, slowly rocking back and forth, her beautiful strawberry blonde locks flowing with the movement, her features resembled those of a fashion model.

Tommy looked at Jimmy. "What?"

"Look at Mrs. Crow."

"Yeah, so?"

"She looks like a witch."

Tommy laughed. "She don't look like any witch I've ever seen. She's gorgeous."

Jimmy lifted his head and looked through the window. When he did, his mouth dropped open, and he felt faint.

"Tommy, I saw her. Before I came downstairs to see you, I saw her. She looked like a witch, honest to God. Cross my heart and hope to die." He finished while making the necessary X in the area of his heart.

"Well, that may be true, but she's no witch now. I gotta go. I'll see you tomorrow."

With that said, Tommy was up and gone, softly closing the door behind him. *How had she done that?* Jimmy thought. *I saw her with my own eyes.*

Over the next few weeks, nothing changed. Every few nights, Mrs. Crow would rock and roll. The never did find Cookies or baby Joey.

It was on a particularly rainy night that it finally happened. Jimmy was looking through the window at Mrs. Crow when she suddenly stood up, turned around, and looked directly at him watching from his window. Jimmy panicked.

"Shitskee, oh, shitskee," he muttered. "I've been caught. I'm really gonna be in trouble now."

Jimmy cautiously raised his head to look over the window sill. To his amazement,

Mr. Crow was standing next to Mrs. Crow, both of them looking right at Jimmy. There was a brilliant flash at the window, Jimmy immediately felt a blast of air that knocked him to the floor.

As he lay there, totally immobilized, he wet himself. The convulsions started slowly at first. Jimmy tried to call out for his mother, but no sounds came from his mouth. After a few moments of convulsing, he vomited, choking on the bitter bile. He couldn't breath. *I'm going to die*, he thought. Tears welled in his eyes. He realized that not only had he lost his playfield and his friends, but now to top it off, he was a goner.

"Breathe slowly." It was Sanora. She placed her hand on his chest, the warmth flowed through his body, the nausea passed, and he could breathe again.

"The time has come, James Michaels, for you to rid your neighborhood of some un-wanted residents. Do you have the paper?"

Jimmy pointed, still unable to speak.

"Get it."

Jimmy obediently went into the closet,

pulled open the door to his secret hiding place and removed the paper. To his great surprise, the writing was complete and totally legible, even in the dark.

Jimmy struggled to speak. "Why not you?"

"You have the strength. You must send them back. Do it now before it's too late."

Jimmy read over the page. There were words he didn't know. He tried to mouth them out.

"Just do your best. Perfection doesn't matter. Only effort and intention."

Jimmy began again, "Infinite creator of all things, hear my prayer. Infinite power of all things, hear my prayer. Infinite harmony of all things, hear my prayer. Yea, the darkness of hades has infested our world. Yea, the sin of the universe has manifested here. Yea, all good must come to the aid of all good. Take those unholy, into darkness. Bring light to this troubled place. Evil be banished. Goodness be restored. Cleanse this space forevermore."

A loud screeching noise, that sounded like a banshee, was howling his name.

Jimmy looked down to see Mr. and Mrs. Crow shaking their fists up at him screaming. "You'll never get rid of us Jimmy Michaels, we'll be back for you!"

Jimmy looked at Sanora. "Now, what?"

"Quick, read the next page."

To his surprise, there was now a second page. He began anew.

"We call to archangel Gabriel and archangel Michael to thrash down the darkness. We plead to the power of Ramtha to wrest this portion of land from the hands of darkness. We command all evil, be gone!"

Jimmy waited for something to happen, but the biggest thing he noticed was how tired he felt.

"Until we meet again, James," Sanora whispered, before vanishing.

The tremendous thunderstorm that followed kept most everyone on Maple awake for the night, though Jimmy was exhausted and slept peacefully. He had slept so soundly that he didn't hear the loud roar caused by the destruction of the house at 1421 Maple. He missed the spinning, twister like wind in the air, and the colorful flash of light that turned the house into vapor. He didn't remember the cursing rages of Mr. and Mrs. Crow as they were drawn back to the lower realms of spirit. He had no knowledge of their vows to return and seek vengeance.

In the morning, Jimmy was startled awake. He was frightened and trembling, but he didn't know why. As a matter of fact, Jimmy felt as though he had experienced a very bad dream.

He looked around the room. Everything seemed normal. There was no little girl, no paper, and no sick feeling. Jimmy slowly dressed, being careful to fold his pajamas, just so. He put on his favorite jeans, his Red Wings jersey, and his Air Jordans.

If he were lucky, his mom would make pancakes. On his way to the kitchen, Jimmy's dad stopped him to relay the good news, Cookies had come home this morning and Joey Franklin was found safe in his crib.

Jimmy heard a knock at the door. It was Tommy.

"Hi, Jimmy. You wanna play ball?"

Jimmy thought for a minute. "Naw, my mom won't let me go to the park."

"The park? What are you, nuts? I can't go to the park either. I just thought we could play in the lot."

Jimmy stepped onto the porch. To his amazement, the house was gone. The ground was back to normal. The cardboard pieces which they used for home plate and the bases were still in their proper places and a brand new football was sitting on home plate. Fourteen twenty-one Maple was his lot again.

Had it all been a long, terrible dream? Was Sanora real? One thing was for certain, they really had caught and eaten all those fish.

For now, it was time to play catch. Jimmy would ask his father later if he knew what happened. He grabbed his glove.

"Mom, I'm gonna head out with Tommy."

Tammy heard her son and answered. "All right, Jimmy. I'll have breakfast ready in a few minutes, Tommy can join us."

Jimmy ran to the center of the lot.

"Throw me a high one, Tommy."

Tommy did his best to lean back and launch the leather sphere high into the air. As a matter of fact, he threw it way over Jimmy's head and into the deep grass near the fence. It took Jimmy a few minutes, but when he finally found it, the ball was resting next to one of the slender wooden sticks with the orange ribbons. The same sticks that surveyors use to mark property for development.

THANK you for reading *1421 Maple*. We hope you enjoyed it! If you'd like to continue The Starlite Supernatural Mystery Series, you can read our standalone shorts in any order.

BOOKS 2 READ

https://books2read.com/ap/nA7AdP/Ray-and-Michele-Fraser

AUTHOR NOTES

Thank you for reading our story.
We love hearing your feedback, so we hope
you'll post a review.

If you liked *1421 Maple*, please check out
our other Starlite Mysteries.

Receive an exciting look into *Mary* by
signing up for our newsletter using the
Bookfunnel link below.
https://dl.bookfunnel.com/xpkhinq30n

Plus, get behind the scenes tidbits and learn
about new releases.

Mary
A young girl with a mysterious background sets off an investigation into the dark reaches of time.

Reviews

Mary
"A short paranormal novella that's just about ninety pages long: I enjoyed every aspect of it. I wished it was longer, but just because I loved the writing style - the characters. The flow of the book was just perfection. Also, I liked the action part at the beginning and the mystery each chapter brought. It never had a dull moment."
- Midnightstorybook

Mary
"Read it as an ARC. Absolutely loved this story. Held my attention the whole time. The plot was consistent from beginning to

end. Gave off a murder mystery vibe without murder. No cliffhangers with a great unexpected ending. Suspenseful and mysterious. Definitely worth reading if you want to try out the supernatural mystery genre."
- <u>Elizabeth S.</u>

Mary
"Every time I thought I had an idea of who Mary was and where she came from, I'd learn about new piece of the puzzle and have to throw all my theories out the window. Things get stranger as the story progresses, which just made me more eager to figure out what was really going on. I felt a bit bad for our main character Jason and his quest to return Mary to her family, but I admired how determined he was to help such an odd little girl.

For such a brief story, "Mary" is packed full of intrigue and mystery - who is this little girl, where is she from, and why doesn't she understand how to drink a milkshake? I can guarantee you won't see the answer coming!

I really enjoyed this read, and I'd recommend it to anyone looking for a novella that will keep them guessing. I'm looking forward to reading more by Ray and Michele Fraser - thank you so much to the authors for the opportunity to read this book!"
- Anna

ALSO BY RAY & MICHELE

If you enjoyed this Starlite Mystery, check out our other unique spellbinding shorts. They're the perfect escape when you're pressed for time.

The Starlite Supernatural Mystery Series:

Haunted

The Wind

The Promise

Mary

1421 Maple

Sarah

Coming Soon

Enter the web of intrigue, suspense, and danger in

The Sean Thomas Paranormal Mystery Series

Book 1 - *A Switch in Time*

For a complete list of Ray and Michele's books

or

to request signed paperbacks visit our website.

www.rayandmichelefraser.com

BOOKS 2 READ

https://books2read.com/ap/nA7AdP/Ray-and-Michele-Fraser

ABOUT THE AUTHORS

Ray and Michele are a full-time writing team with a serious passion for storytelling. They combine their love of writing, vivid imagination, and years of experience as professional spirit mediums to guide their readers into uncharted territories.

In 1994, Ray's intuitions fostered by Cherokee and Scottish ancestry, led him to open Mystiques-West Metaphysical Center in Michigan. During the twenty-three years of operation, Ray hosted a #1 radio talk show and a live TV show, called "The Mystical Connection." They performed home cleansing, organized ghost hunts, taught classes in mediumship, and led weekly public seances to connect clients to their departed loved ones on the other side. The messages from spirit have helped many to find peace. Ray also facilitated the last four National Houdini Seances sponsored by Houdini historian Sid Radner.

In addition to readings and life coaching sessions, Ray's work as an ordained minister has provided his clientele with years of grief and relationship counseling, weddings, and funerals.

As a screenwriter, Michele brings her love of film into the fold by incorporating her own style of creativity into their endeavors. She's also the backbone of the editing process, social media management, cover design, and marketing.

Ray and Michele infuse their stories with mystery, intrigue, tales of the afterlife, and other worldly phenomena to create a fascinating and adventurous journey for readers.

For more info -
linktr.ee/RayandMicheleFraser

Ray's extensive background and keen storytelling abilities combined with Michele's love of screenwriting and editing has made them a powerhouse duo. www.rayandmichelefraser.com

instagram.com/rayandmichelefraser

facebook.com/RayandMicheleFraser

x.com/RandMFraser

youtube.com/@HiddenDoorPressLosAngeles

DON'T MISS OUT

Click the button below to sign up for our fan exclusive newsletter to get behind the scenes tidbits and learn about new book releases.

There's no charge or obligation,
and we never sell your information.

https://rayandmichelefraser.com/
newsletter

BOOKS 2 READ

https://books2read.com/ap/nA7AdP/Ray-and-Michele-Fraser

WHAT PEOPLE ARE SAYING

Haunted

"Ray and Michele do not disappoint. I could not put this book down. It left me wanting to know more. I'm a big fan of haunted houses and was very intrigued with this story. I honestly didn't see the story going the way it did. I actually felt as if I was there. I felt all the emotions the characters felt. I'm still in awe at the story and cannot wait until their next book!!"
- Shana L.

The Wind

"This book ensnared me from the get-go. Like the wind whispering encouragement to keep on reading. The fact that the writers are able to create such a wonderfully thrilling story within such few pages is pure magic. It kept me on my toes and I read the whole thing in one sitting. I genuinely believe this could be adapted into a full length novel.

Character development was great especially for a novella and the storyline was stella.

I would highly recommend this, and during the start it was giving me major Phantom vibes by Dean R Koontz and he is one of my all time favs in the thriller department.

If you like thrillers, or wives tales or simply short stories then this is the book for you, even if you only said yes to one of those."
- Juniper Raven

The Promise
"Just finished reading this story... and I am blessed beyond words! It's a beautiful paranormal novella focusing on grief, loss, sadness, and ultimately - redemption. For lovers of *Chicken Soup for the Soul* books and the *Sixth Sense* film, you will be delighted to have the time to read this short story - and feel compelled to engage in the entire series! Thank you to @rayandmichelefraser for the

wonderful opportunity to share this story of mystery and intrigue with you all! I highly recommend and rate it 5 of 5 sweet stars!"
- Deb

Mary
"I went into this novella only knowing that it was described as a paranormal mystery. I love paranormal books but I don't read mystery too often so I was interested to see how these two genres combined. Immediately as the story began I was interested in discovering who exactly this mysterious Mary was. I thought I had an idea as to where things were going and who Mary was but I was so wrong! I don't want to spoil anything, but when Jason started digging up the past I certainly didn't expect the story to go where it did. This was a quick yet captivating read that I'd recommend if you're a fan of either paranormal or mystery."
- MissS3LFD3STRUKT

Sarah
"This is a page turner. Sarah finds herself in a destructive marriage that is not at all what she thought she was getting into. Charlie is charming on the outside with an evil heart. To survive, she had to do something drastic. But will she ever be truly free from her torturing husband? Fans of A Tell Tale Heart will find this an interesting twist on a classic story."
- Brook